BORED TO DEATH

A NOIR-OTIC STORY

Jonathan Ames

Scribner
New York London Toronto Sydney

SCRIBNER
A Division of Simon & Schuster, Inc.
1230 Avenue of the Americas
New York, NY 10020

This Scribner edition October 2009

For information about special discounts for bulk purchases, please contact Simon & Schuster Special Sales at 1-866-506-1949 or business@simonandschuster.com.

The Simon & Schuster Speakers Bureau can bring authors to your live event. For more information or to book an event contact the Simon & Schuster Speakers Bureau at 1-866-248-3049 or visit our website at www.simonspeakers.com.

Manufactured in the United States of America

10   9   8   7   6   5   4   3   2   1

ISBN 978-1-4391-8437-0
ISBN 978-1-4391-8403-5 (ebook)

For Ray Pitt

BORED TO DEATH

The trouble happened because I was bored. At the time, I was twenty-eight days sober. I was spending my nights playing Internet backgammon. I should have been going to AA meetings, but I wasn't.

I had been going to AA meetings for twenty years, ever since college. I like AA meetings. My problem is that I'm a periodic alcoholic, even with going to AA. Every few years, I try drinking again. Or, rather, drinking tries me. It tries me on for size and finds out I don't fit and throws me to the ground. And so I go crawling back to AA. Or at least I should. This last go-round, I was skipping meetings and just staying home and, like I said, playing Internet backgammon.

I was also reading a lot of crime fiction and private detective fiction, writers like Hammett, Goodis, Chandler, Thompson. The usual suspects, as it were. Since my own life was so dull, I needed the charge that came from their books—the danger, the violence, the despair.

So that's all I was doing—reading and playing backgammon. I can afford such a lifestyle because I'm a writer. I'm not a hugely successful writer, but I'm my own boss. I've written six books—three novels and three essay collections—and at the time of the trouble I had roughly six thousand dollars in the bank, which is a lot for me. I also had a few checks for movie work coming in down the road.

By my economic standards it was a flush time. I had even paid my taxes early, at the end of March—it was now mid-April—and I was just trying to stay sober and keep a low profile in my own little life. I wasn't doing any writing, because, well, I didn't have anything to say.

Overall, I was being pretty reclusive. I only talked to a few people, primarily my parents, who are retired and live in Florida and who call me every day. They're a bit needy, my senior citizen parents, but I don't mind, life is short, so if I can give them a little solace with a daily call, what the hell. My father is eighty-two and my mother is seventy-five. I have to love them now as best I can. And the only other two people I really spoke to were the two close friends I have, one who lives here in New York and the other who's in Los Angeles. I have a lot of acquaintances, but I've never had a lot of friends.

One night a week, I did leave the apartment to go see this girl. It was nice. I guess you could say that she was a friend, too, but I've never really thought of the women in my life as friends, which must be a flaw. Her name was Marie and we would have dinner, maybe go to a movie, and then we'd get into bed at her place, never my place, and the sex with her was good. But it wasn't anything serious. She was twenty-six and I'm forty-two, and I retired from being serious with women a few years ago. Somebody always got hurt, usually the girl, and I couldn't take it anymore.

Well, I'll shut up now about all this. It's not my drinking problem or my finances or my dead love life that I want to talk about. I only mention all this as some kind of way to explain why I had too much free time on my hands, because what's really on my mind is this trouble I got into because, as I said, I was bored. Bored with backgammon and bored with reading and bored with being sober and bored with myself and bored with being alive.

I should make it clear that I wasn't at all bored by the books I was tearing through and loving, but bored by the fact that I wasn't actually doing anything, just reading, though it was, in fact, Hammett and Goodis and Chandler and Thompson who sort of provoked me to take action, and it's when I took action, because of those authors' books, that I blew up my life.

It was a fantasy, a crazed notion, but I got it into my head that I wanted to play at being a private detective. I wanted to help somebody. I wanted to be brave. I wanted to have an adventure. And it's pathetic, but what did I do? I put an ad on craigslist in the "services" section under "legal." It read as follows:

Private Detective for Hire
Reply to: serv-261446940@craigslist.org
Date: 2007–04–13, 8:31AM EST

Specializing: Missing Persons, Domestic Issues.
I'm not licensed, but maybe I'm someone who can help you. My fee is reasonable.
Call 347-555-1042

There were two other private-detective ads on craigslist and they offered all sorts of help—surveillance, undercover work, background checks, video and still photography, business investigations, missing persons, domestic issues, and two things that I didn't quite grasp—"skip tracing" and "witness locates."

I figured the only thing I could help with was trying to find someone or maybe following someone, which would most likely be a "domestic issue"—an unfaithful spouse or boyfriend or girlfriend. I didn't have any qualms about that, following an unfaithful lover, though in all the private-detective fiction I've read the heroes never do "marriage work," as if it's beneath them, but I thought it would be fun to follow somebody and to do so for the purposes of a real mission. Sometimes, probably because I want everything to be like it is in a book or a movie, I have followed people on the streets of New York, pretending I was a detective or a spy.

I did try to cover myself legally by writing in my ad that I wasn't licensed. I don't know who does license private detectives, but I figured it was a difficult process and, anyway, I just wanted to put the ad up, mostly as a lark, a playing-out of a dream, like when I would shadow people on the streets. But I really didn't think anybody would actually call me—I was offering far fewer services than the other private detectives and I was acknowledging in the ad that I wasn't exactly a professional.

If somebody did call, then I figured after talking to me they would try somebody more reputable, but whatever came of it, even if nobody called, I thought it might be something I could write about, a comedic essay—"My Failed Attempt at Being a Private Detective." Often during my writing career, mostly for my essays, I've put myself in weird positions and then milked it for humor. This situation would be like the time I tried to go to an orgy but wasn't allowed in. Even when nothing happens, you can sometimes make a good story out of it.

Anyway, I got a thrill at posting the ad, but it was a short-lived thrill. For the first day, I would go and look at my ad, admiring my own handiwork, laughing to myself, wondering if something might happen, almost as if I checked it out enough times, other people would. But then, after about a day, the thrill wore off. It was one more ridiculous thing in a ridiculous life, and, of course, no one called.

So I went back to the usual routine—I started a David Goodis novel, *Black Friday*, and once again I was spending hours playing backgammon. Then on Thursday, April 19, when I was in the midst of a good game, my cell phone rang around four o'clock in the afternoon. The number had an area code I couldn't immediately place—215. I answered the phone and kept on playing.

"Hello?" I said.

"I saw your ad," said a girl's voice.

"What? What ad?" I said. I had forgotten completely about my craigslist posting. It had been six days.

"Craigslist? Missing persons?"

"Yes, of course, I'm sorry," I said, quickly rallying, remembering my little experiment. "I was distracted. I'm sorry. And most of my clients are word-of-mouth, so I forgot about my ad on craigslist. How can I help you?"

Right away, I was trying to sound professional, and the lie about the other clients just came to me naturally. I've always been a good liar.

"It's about my sister . . ." she started to say, then hesitated, and I glanced at my laptop, at the game. If I resigned, which is the same thing as losing and at the moment I was ahead, my ranking would go down, and I hate for my ranking to go down. I've worked very hard to get it to the second-highest level. I was momentarily conflicted, but I clicked a button and resigned from the game so that I could give my full attention to this other game, this one with the young-sounding girl on the phone.

"Your sister?" I said, prompting her.

"Well, I came in from Philadelphia this morning"—she started slow and then her speech came fast, real fast, the way young girls talk—"and we're supposed to go to a show tonight. I know it's weird but we got tickets to *Beauty and the Beast*, we saw it when we were really young and loved it and now it's closing, so that's why we want to see it, but she didn't answer her phone all day yesterday or this morning, but I came in anyway, it was our plan, I figured she's just not picking up or it's not charged, she always forgets to charge her phone, but she's still not answering and now her voice mail is full, and no one at her dorm has seen her for a while and the guard let me in, but she's not in her room, the door is locked, she has a single, and I don't want to call my parents and freak them out, but I have a weird feeling, she's got this sleazy boyfriend, and I don't know what to do, and I'm at this Internet café and I always use craigslist for everything, so I typed in 'missing persons' and found you."

This was a lot to digest. I tried to break it down.

"Your sister lives in a dorm? Where?"

"Twelfth Street and Third Avenue. It's an NYU dorm."

"And where are you?" I asked.

"This café. On Second Avenue. I don't know the cross street, let me look out the window . . . Third Street."

"What's your name?"

"Rachel."

"Last name?"

"Weiss."

"Your sister's name?"

"Lisa . . . Weiss."

"And I'm Jonathan . . . Spencer, by the way . . . You can call me Jonathan. And you live in Philadelphia?" The lies were coming fast and easy. Spencer was my strange middle name. I'm Jewish but my parents loaded me up with a WASP assembly of names, Jonathan Spencer Ames.

"Yeah, I go to Temple," she said. "I'm a freshman."

"What year is your sister?"

"Junior."

"And where are your parents?"

"Maryland . . . Can you help me? I don't have anywhere to stay tonight, if I can't find her, and she has the tickets to *Beauty and the Beast*, and so I think I should just go back to Philly but I'm not sure what to do."

"I think I can help you. I can come meet you in about thirty minutes. I'm in Brooklyn, but it's a very quick subway ride. I know the café you are in . . . I charge one hundred dollars a day, but I bet I can find her by tonight or at least tomorrow. Can you afford a down payment of at least one hundred dollars to cover the first day?"

"Yes," she said. "I have money. I can go to an ATM."

"Just wait at the café. I'll be there in thirty minutes. Maybe twenty . . . What do you look like?"

"Why?"

"So I can recognize you."

"Oh . . . I have dark hair, almost black. Kind of long. I'm wearing a yellow dress and a kind of thick white sweater."

"Okay . . . I'll have a tan cap on. Not to frighten you, but my most distinctive feature is my white eyebrows. I'm not an albino. The sun has bleached them over the years. I'll be there by four thirty."

"I guess so," she said, a bit nonsensically. Her voice was practically a whisper. She wasn't sure she was doing the right thing. I cursed myself for possibly blowing it with the mention of the white eyebrows and sounding like a nut.

"Everything will be okay. I'll find your sister," I said.

"All right," she said meekly.

"See you in a little bit," I said, and hung up, before she changed her mind.

I put on a tie, loosened it at the collar, and undid the top button to give myself a rumpled, world-weary private-detective look, and I threw on my gray-tweed Brooks Brothers sport coat, since there was a slight chill in the air. Also, on all the covers of my Chandler novels, Philip Marlowe, the great private detective, is always wearing a sport coat. Then, so the girl would recognize me, I put on my cap, and I usually wear a hat of some kind, anyway, since I'm bald and buzz my hair down, and without hair it's a very drafty world. I was already wearing my favorite olive green corduroy pants and looking at myself in the mirror, I felt, overall, quite capable of finding this missing NYU coed, at least wardrobe-wise.

I grabbed *Black Friday* to read in the subway and was out of the apartment within five minutes of hanging up the phone.

The café had uncomfortable aluminum chairs and we sat with our legs practically touching. She was a cute little thing—very white skin and very dark hair. Her mind was soft, though, and that cut down the attraction and made it easier to keep my attention focused on the business at hand. I got the following information out of her, expanding on what she had told me on the phone: the sister, Lisa, about a year ago, had disappeared for a week with an older boyfriend (early thirties) and the family had gone into a panic; now she had a different boyfriend, but the same genus—thirtysomething, guitarist in a rock band, a bartender, and possibly a junkie; Rachel didn't want to get the parents or the police or NYU security involved, because it was probably nothing and her sister would kill her if she blew the whistle; at the same time, she had a bad feeling—she was worried that her sister had maybe starting using heroin.

I figured the boyfriend was the key to this whole thing and she told me his name was Vincent, but she didn't have a last name. He worked at a bar called Lakes on Avenue B. Rachel, on an earlier trip to the city, had gone there with her sister. The NYU students liked it because the place was lax when it came to asking for proof of age.

"Do you have a picture of Lisa?" I asked.

"No," she said. Then she remembered that her sister had sent a picture of herself with Vincent to her cell phone. From Vincent's cell phone. This was a coup—I had a picture and a number to work with. She showed me the picture—Lisa was more severe than her sister, high cheekbones, a sensual mouth, but the same dark hair and marble white skin. Vincent had a yellow, long face, a tattoo of some kind on his neck, and a false look of rock-band confidence in his eyes.

I called Vincent's number and his voice mail, like Lisa's, was full. But at least I had a number. I suggested to Rachel that we go over to Kinko's on Astor Place and that she e-mail me the picture and we print it up.

But first we called the sister, on the off chance that this could be solved right here and now and the two girls could go see *Beauty and the Beast* as planned and live happily ever after. Not unexpectedly, the call went right to the filled-up voice mail. So then we swung by the dorm, with the same hope of an easy resolution, but the sister still wasn't in her room. I instructed Rachel to ask the guard in an offhand way if he had seen her sister—she showed him the cell phone picture—and he said he hadn't.

It was now almost five thirty and as we walked over to

Kinko's, I said, giving her an out and giving me an out, "Are you really sure you don't want to go to the cops or let your parents know?"

"I'm sure," she said. "Lisa'll go ballistic. She's probably forgot about the play and is just having sex for hours. Somebody told me that if you do heroin you just keep having sex and don't want to stop."

"I think that's crystal meth," I said, "but I could be wrong." My problems have always been with alcohol and cocaine, so I wasn't too sure about these other drugs.

"Whatever," she said. "I don't even like beer. She always goes with the worst guys possible. He's either shooting her up with heroin or giving her crystal meth. It's like it turns her on to find a serial killer or something."

We stopped at the Chase Bank on Astor Place and she gave me one hundred dollars. At Kinko's, I printed up a blurry but recognizable portrait of the two lovebirds.

At Fourth Avenue, we waited for a cab to take her to Penn Station and from there she'd catch the next train to Philly.

"Are you really a professional?" she asked.

"I'm not licensed," I said, "but I've been at this a while." I had been reading pulp fiction off and on for years. It was an apprenticeship of sorts and was the little bit of truth that made the lie sound sincere. I may have been having a bipolar episode. "The first thing I'm going to do is find Vincent and when I find Vincent, I'll find your sister."

She got in a cab and as I closed the door, I said, "I'll call you later tonight."

"Okay," she said, and she looked scared and dumb. But she was a sweet kid. The cab drove off and the six o'clock light was beautiful, day darkening into night.

I stood on the corner and called information and got the number for Lakes Bar.

"Lakes." It was a woman's voice, young-sounding. I could hear a jukebox in the background.

"Is Vincent there?" I asked. "The bartender."

"He comes in after me, at eight," she said. "Works eight to four."

"Okay, thanks . . . Listen, I owe him some money and I'm going to bring him by a check. Can you spell his last name for me?"

"What? Yeah. I know. It's a weird name. I'm pretty sure there are two *t*'s. E-T-T-I-N."

"Thanks so much," I said, and hung up.

People will give you anything if you just ask directly. I called information and there was only one Vincent Ettin listed in Manhattan, and this Ettin still had a landline and lived at 425 West Forty-seventh Street. I had two hours to kill before he was to be at work at eight. Maybe I could find him beforehand, so I called the number and got an answering machine. It was a no-nonsense message: "This is Vincent. You know what to do." It could have been the guy in the picture or some other Vincent Ettin. I didn't leave a message.

I walked over to West Eighth Street and took the A train up to Forty-second Street. When I got out of the subway the last of the light was gone and it was evening; 425 was an old five-story walk-up. Apartment 4F had the name Ettin next to the buzzer. I buzzed 4F. Nothing. I buzzed 2F. A voice, that of an old lady, came through the intercom: "Who is it?"

"Building inspector, let me in."

"Who?"

"City building inspector, fire codes, let me in."

The door buzzed open. I went up to the fourth floor. I knocked at 4F. No answer. I knocked again. Silence. Out of instinct I didn't know I had, I tried the doorknob and the place was unlocked. Heart pounding with the feeling of transgression, I stepped in, the lights were on, and I called out "Hello," like a fool, and then I got hit by a bad smell. There were two large mounds of shit on the floor, right near the door, and I nearly stepped on them. There was also a pool of piss, which I *had* stepped in. *What the hell is this?* I thought. I closed the door and again called out, "Hello?"

I stepped over the shit and the piss, and separate from those two grosser elements it was definitely a ragged dump of a place and reminded me of my own apartment. There was a futon couch with white hairs all over it, an old TV, a good-looking stereo, a cluttered coffee table, and at the far end a miniature, nasty New York kitchen. There were no pictures anywhere, so I had no idea if this was the apartment of the Vincent Ettin that I was looking for.

A little black-and-white mutt came from some back room off the kitchen, probably the bedroom. Its tail was between its legs and it looked defeated and humiliated. Not much of a watchdog, it came over to me and I petted its head. I went through the kitchen and looked in the bedroom—nobody was there, just an unmade futon bed, and a lot of musical equipment, several amps and three guitars, all of it new and expensive-looking. The bathroom, which was off the bedroom, was a squalid closet and also empty of human life.

The dog was following me around and I got the idea that if he hadn't been walked for a while, at least two days for the two dumps, he also probably hadn't been fed. I found a bowl and dry dog food in the kitchen and set him up. Then I headed for the front door and I noticed two things—the window behind the futon-couch was wide-open with no screen and it led to a fire escape, which would make the place pretty vulnerable to a break-in, though the unlocked door made things even easier, and I also saw that there was a cell phone on the coffee table.

The musical equipment had pretty much convinced me that this was the V. Ettin I was looking for, but then to confirm it I called the cell number I had for him and the phone on the coffee table vibrated but didn't ring. The dog looked up but then kept on eating, and the phone moving on the coffee table, like a living thing, gave me a spooked feeling. So I hung up my phone, but Ettin's phone, because of some delay in the system, still shuddered, like something twitching before dying, until it finally did stop. Then I got the hell out of there.

I took the train back downtown and then made the long walk east over to Avenue B. By the time I got to Lakes, which was at the corner of Eleventh, it was eight thirty. It was a dark, stripped-down place. It had a scarred wood bar, plenty of booze, three taps for beer, stools, some booths, and a jukebox. It wasn't too crowded, and there was a man behind the bar but it wasn't Ettin. This fellow was short and very skinny and had a shiny, shaved head. My head is shaved but I always leave it stubbly, using old-fashioned barber's clippers. This guy went at his head with a razor.

I took a stool and for a moment I thought of ordering a beer. I wavered, then regained the old sober thinking, and when the bartender came over to me, I ordered a club soda. I gave him three bucks, sipped my drink, and he took care of some other customers. I wondered if Ettin was running late or wasn't going to show up. I waited a few minutes, then I waved the bartender over, deciding to show him my full hand. I took out the picture of Lisa Weiss and Vincent Ettin, which I'd folded up and put in the Goodis novel.

"Do you know these two?"

"Yeah," he said, wary. "What's this about?"

"What are their names?"

"That's Vincent and Lisa. What the fuck is going on?"

"I've been hired by Lisa's family to find her. She's been missing for a few days and she doesn't answer her phone and neither does Vincent. Do you know where they might be?"

The bartender looked at me and then looked down the bar and out the window by the front door, not for any real reason except to avoid my eye. I took forty dollars out of my wallet and put it on the bar. I don't know who I thought I was, but I had all the moves. Shiny-head saw the money.

"Tell me what you know," I said.

"Lisa is missing?"

"Yes, and her family is very concerned."

"Well . . . okay, I don't know where she is. Vince was supposed to work tonight but he called me a few hours ago and asked me to cover for him. He said he was upstate, that his band had a gig in Buffalo."

"Buffalo?"

"That's what he said. But my phone has caller ID and it said that he was calling from the Senton Hotel and it was a 212 number, Manhattan."

"What do you think he's doing at the Senton?"

"He might be on a run."

"Drugs?"

"Yeah. He was on methadone but he went off about a month ago. First he was just snorting lines and then he started shooting it again."

Shiny realized that maybe he was saying too much, he was a natural gossip and hadn't been able to help himself. I pushed the forty over to him.

"I appreciate the information," I said.

"I'm only telling you all this because of Lisa. She's a young kid." He looked down at the forty bucks, which he still hadn't touched.

"I hear you," I said.

"What are you going to do?" he asked.

"Go to the Senton. That's probably where Lisa is."

I sat up from the stool. Shiny pocketed the forty and said, "Listen, before you came in another guy was looking for Vincent and gave me his card to give to Vincent. You'll probably see him before I do, so here's the card."

He pulled the card out of his pocket and handed it to me. On the card was the letter *G* in the middle and a 917 number. Below the number, handwritten, was *4/20/2007*, which would be the next day.

"So you didn't know this guy?"

"No."

"What was he like?"

"Spanish. A tough guy. About your height, six foot, but he looked like he lifted weights."

"How old?"

"My age. Thirties. To be honest, he kind of scared me."

I went outside, got the Senton's number, and called. They had no Vincent Ettin registered, but that didn't mean anything. I knew the Senton. It was on Twenty-eighth Street and Broadway and it was a flop hotel. Unless they were stupid, people didn't give their real names when they registered. You only went to the Senton to do drugs and hide out with prostitutes. It was run, like most flop hotels, by Indians. I knew the place because in the mid-nineties I had a booze and coke relapse and holed up there myself for two days with a prostitute. For some reason, you never want to do such things in your own home. Better to go on a run in an anonymous hotel room, and then when it's over you walk away and don't have to clean up the mess. I figured if the Senton was still in business, it probably hadn't changed much.

I got a taxi and in the ride over to the hotel, I tried Lisa Weiss's number for the hell of it and got her filled-up voice mail. I called both of Vincent Ettin's numbers, just in case he had returned to Forty-seventh Street, but no luck on that end. I thought of that sweet dog alone in the apartment. It had nice eyes.

The Senton hadn't changed and neither had that stretch of Twenty-eighth Street. All of Manhattan is being turned into one big glossy, high-end mall, but Twenty-eighth Street was still a dark and empty corridor, at least at night, and had an illicit feeling to it that was kind of comforting, like you couldn't drain all the life out of New York, even if that life was the kind that was trying to kill itself.

The Senton was just as I remembered it. It didn't have much in the way of a lobby, more of a narrow hallway, with a small alcove off to the right with one old stuffed chair and at the end of the hallway there was an Indian in an office, behind a thick bulletproof piece of glass, with an opening at the bottom of the glass for the passing back and forth of money and keys. Past the office was the beat-up-looking door to the elevator.

I approached the office and the Indian, a pockmarked, exhausted-looking fellow, said he hadn't seen the two people in the picture, which I held up to the glass, but even if he had I don't think he would have told me. I asked him if I could wait in the alcove in case they were in the hotel and I could talk to them if and when they headed out. I explained to him that I very much needed to find them, the young girl in particular.

"You could wait there, if you rent a room," he said. "It's sixty dollars for three hours, ninety for the night."

I thought of just staking out the place from the sidewalk, but I didn't know how long I would be out there and it was a bit cold, even for an April night. I decided to rent the room for three hours, see if I got lucky. Between my tip for Shiny back at the bar, not to mention the subway rides and the cab, I was losing money on this deal, not that I was in it for the money, but still. I kicked myself for not telling Rachel that there would be expenses. What had I been thinking? Marlowe always quoted a day rate *plus expenses*.

Anyway, I registered as Philip Marlowe and got the key to my room but I didn't go up to it. I went and sat in the alcove. If Vincent and Lisa headed out to get something to eat or go for cigarettes, I would be right there. I took out my Goodis novel and started reading, looking up from the page every few minutes when somebody walked past me, which meant I was eyeballing a variety of prostitutes—females, trannies, gay hustlers—and the usual ragged assortment of middle-aged married johns, plus other sundry types who were using the Senton just to party.

I read for about an hour, and then I put the book down and kind of meditated, mulling things over, trying to make sense of it—Lisa, the pretty girl in the picture with the dark hair and beautiful mouth; Vincent's empty apartment with the dog shit and the left-behind cell phone and the open window and the unlocked door; and this card from "G" with tomorrow's date written on it. In the midst of all this cogitating, my parents called. My mother had taken a t'ai chi class for seniors at the Y and my father's ring finger had bent in and he couldn't straighten it out.

We eventually rang off, and I thought some more about my "case." I didn't know what to make of anything, but in my own sick way I was having a good time. Then around eleven p.m., after sitting there for nearly two hours, I really had to go to the bathroom. I wasn't sure what to do about this. I couldn't recall Marlowe or Hammett's detective, the Continental Op, having to give up a stakeout position because of the toilet. What if during the time I was in the bathroom, I missed the two I was looking for? That would be bad luck, and from playing backgammon, I know that you get a lot of bad luck when you play a game. Mostly I had been rolling good—Ettin being listed and the door not being locked at his apartment, the bartender having caller ID and being willing to feed me plenty of information. So it was all the more reason why something should go against me.

I went back to the Indian behind the glass. I asked him if there was a toilet on the ground floor that I could use.

"No," he said. "You have a toilet in your room."

"All right, listen," I said, and I took the picture back out and again pressed it to the glass, "if these two come out while I'm in the bathroom, tell them there's someone here that needs to see them. Stall them for me."

"Fuck you," he said, but it wasn't a "fuck you" with malice. It was primarily a simple statement of refusal. It was vulgar, but there was room for negotiation.

I took twenty dollars out of my wallet and slid it through the movie-ticket opening at the bottom of the glass. He took the money and didn't say anything, but I thought he would do what I had asked.

I walked quickly over to the elevator, waited a good long time for it—and I really needed to piss—and then I rode the

thing at a glacial speed up to my room on the fifth floor. The
room was clean enough, cigarette burns on most every surface,
but the bed was made and there was one towel in the bathroom.
I took a piss and felt profound relief. Sometimes a good piss is
incredible.

I took the elevator back down, again waiting at least three minutes for it, and returned to the lobby. I had been gone about ten
minutes, mostly because of the elevator. I went up to the glass.
"You didn't see them, did you?"

"I saw the man," he said. "He came in right after you left and
went up to his room."

"Shit. Came in? You mean, he didn't go out? And the girl wasn't
with him?"

"Yeah, he came in. And no girl."

"So he went up to his room. That's excellent. What's his room
number?"

"Fuck you."

"I need to talk to this guy," I said. "I'm a good person. I'm looking for this young girl for her family. I'm not going to make any
trouble."

"Fuck you."

I took out another twenty and slid it through.

"Sixty-three," he said.

I waited nearly five minutes for the elevator and thought of
walking up the stairs, but then kept on waiting. Finally, it came. I
went up to the sixth floor, another long ride. I knocked at sixty-
three and got no response. I could hear the TV playing inside, and
playing in the other rooms on the hall. I knocked again, but with
more force. I said, through the door, "I have a note for you from
G." I thought that might rouse him. I waited. I put my ear against
the door and didn't hear any movement. I tried the knob. Vincent
Ettin was not big on locking doors. I let myself in. He was lying
on the big queen-size bed, his arms splayed out. There was a band
of rubber wrapped around Vincent's right arm and there was a
needle still in his left hand.

I had never seen a dead body in my forty-two years and Vincent Ettin was my first.

Near a deli on Seventh Avenue and Twenty-eighth was a pay phone. It didn't work. I walked a few blocks south and found one that did work. It had been years since I used a pay phone. I called 911 and reported a dead body in the Senton Hotel on Twenty-eighth Street, room sixty-three. The operator wanted my name and I hung up. I called 911 again, spoke to a different operator, and told that person the same thing and hung up. I wanted to make sure they got it right.

Fifteen minutes before those phone calls, I had been in his room, just staring at the body, terrified and disbelieving, but then I'd had the presence of mind to close the door and I got on the bed right next to him. I cursed myself for not knowing CPR. *Do I pinch his nostrils and blow into his mouth? Do I pound on his chest?* His eyes were open, but they were like the eyes of a doll. I felt his neck for a pulse, feeling the skin beneath the tattoo, which was some obscure Asian markings, and there wasn't anything there, no pulse, no life. Then I put my head against his chest and I couldn't hear anything. But I opened his lips, anyway, and held his nose shut—it's what I had seen on TV—and I suppressed a scream of terror and blew air into him. I thought I might be sick. I did it for maybe twenty seconds and it had no effect. I pulled away. My first animal instinct had been correct—he was dead.

I staggered out of the room, sort of trembly and dizzy, but I walked down the six flights of stairs to get my head straight, and then went right out of the hotel, not handing in my key, not saying anything to my Indian pal. Just got out of there. Let him try to find Philip Marlowe.

After making the 911 calls and walking about twenty blocks in some kind of frenzied panic, spitting repeatedly to get the taste of the dead man out of my mouth, I hailed a cab to take me back to Brooklyn. In the car, I tried calling Lisa Weiss, hoping to end this nightmare and find the damn girl, but got the same fucking filled-up voice mail. I then tried calling Rachel Weiss, but she didn't pick up and I left a message, saying she should call me right away, though I tried to keep my voice calm. When I spoke to her, I was going to tell her to have her parents call the police right away. But I have to say, this scared me. What kind of trouble could I get into for taking on this whole thing and then anonymously reporting a dead body? But it didn't matter, I just had to get out of this mess.

I got home around twelve thirty and lay on top of my bed for hours, didn't even take off my sport coat or shoes, just lay there, numb, waiting for Rachel to call, but she never did. At some point, I passed out. I woke up around eight a.m. and called Rachel again and left another voice mail. At nine I tried her again and I got a recording telling me that the service at the number had been suspended. Fucking college student hadn't paid her bill and I needed to talk to her!

I thought of calling her parents but I didn't know where in Maryland they lived. I started pacing in my dirty apartment. I went on craigslist and called one of the private detectives listed. I told him most of my story, kept it real tight, except I didn't say anything about my bogus ad, just that I was a friend trying to help out.

"Why did you make an anonymous call to the cops?" the PI asked. He had a gruff voice.

"I don't know. I was scared."

"That doesn't look good. Makes it seem like you did something wrong. You and your friend better go to the police. It sounds like you stepped in a big pile of shit."

"Could you help us?" I asked. I hadn't told him about Vincent's dog, so he didn't know how accurate his metaphor was.

He was silent a moment, then he said, "I'm busy," and he hung up. He must not have liked the sound of the whole thing. I didn't blame him.

I tried Rachel's number again and got the same recording. I called Temple University information and the number they had for her was her cell phone.

Stay cool, I told myself. *Stay cool.* I undressed and took a shower.

I dried off and got dressed in the same clothes I had been wearing, except for the tie. Putting on fresh clothes seemed like too much to ask of myself. I tried Rachel and her sister just to torture myself, got the usual results, and I even thought for a moment of calling Vincent's number, and then I remembered that he was dead. I was already unraveled and it was getting worse.

I sat at my desk, staring at the computer, and I thought of calling the cops or going to the cops, my local precinct, but what would I say? I had posted a bogus ad, then given a false name to some undergrad from Temple University, run around the city, found a dead body, and made two anonymous calls to 911.

I filled my kettle to boil some water to make coffee in my French press. Marlowe was always making himself coffee. The thing to do was to stay calm and not overreact, that's how Marlowe always handled himself. While the water did its thing, I started dialing 911 again, to get this over with, but then I couldn't go through with it. I was too scared. I hung up the phone.

I poured myself a cup of coffee and sat back down at my desk, like it was any other day, and because I'm a sick person, I logged on to the backgammon site, thinking that a game might clear my head, and on the site the day was listed: April 20, 2007. I didn't start playing. I remembered the card from G. I took it out of my wallet. I held it, and sipped my coffee.

There were two competing thoughts in my head: (1) go to the cops right now, and (2) call G. Calling G had the appeal of a first drink on a relapse. You know you're going horribly against the grain, doing the wrong thing, what they call in the AA *Big Book* "a sickening rebellion," but there's some kind of mad force of nature that makes you do it, that demands that you do it. So before I could stop myself, in the grips of it, the impulse to self-destruct, to get deeper into this mess, I dialed *67 to block my number and then dialed the number on the card.

"Yeah." It was a deep voice. I was going off the deep end, but for once at least I didn't get somebody's fucking voice mail and that was a relief.

"Is this G?" I asked.

"Who's this?" There was some trace of a Spanish accent, but not much. "How'd you get my number?"

"I . . . I went to Lakes Bar, the bartender gave me your card. I've been looking for the girlfriend of Vincent Ettin. Lisa Weiss. Do you, by any chance, know where she is?"

"Where's Vincent at? Who is this?"

"Do you think you can help me?"

"What the fuck are you talking about? Help you with what?" The voice was angry, hostile, fierce.

"Finding this girl."

"Where's Vincent. I need to speak to him."

"This is going to sound strange. I don't know if you're good friends. But he's dead."

"What the fuck you saying?"

"I was looking for this girl, Lisa Weiss, and I found Vincent. He was in a hotel and he OD'd."

"This is fucked-up. You're a friend of Vincent's? Where are you?"

"I'm not a friend. I'm looking for the girl."

"How do you know he's dead if you're not a friend."

"I found him dead."

"You're fucking lying to me. Who are you? Tell me your fucking name."

"Jonathan Spencer. Do you know where the girl is?"

"Okay," he said, less heated. He was suddenly all calm and gentle. "I know Lisa. She's a friend. She's a good girl. You and I should meet up and talk this out. Figure out what is going on. Where do you live?"

"I'm in Brooklyn, but I'll meet you somewhere. Where are you?"

"I'm in Brooklyn. Red Hook. Come to where I work. You know Coffey Street, off of Van Brunt? You know Red Hook?"

"Yeah, it's not far from me. Where do you work?"

"C and L."

"What's C and L?"

"Beverage distributor."

"Okay . . . How about we meet at this restaurant in Red Hook—Hope and Anchor, you know that place? It's open for breakfast."

"Yeah, sure, I know it. We deliver to them."

"Want to meet there in half an hour?"

"Okay."

"And you'll tell me where Lisa is?"

"Yeah. Yeah."

"Can you just tell me on the phone, then?"

"Listen you f—" He reigned himself in. "I want to talk to you about Vincent, this shit about OD'ing. It's not something to talk about on the phone, hearing that someone you know is dead, if he is dead. So let's meet up and talk this shit out."

"All right, see you at the restaurant in half an hour. I'll be wearing a tan cap and a gray sport coat."

"I'll find you," he said, and hung up.

Like somebody sleepwalking and going out a ten-story window, not knowing what they're doing, I called Promenade car service, the one I always use. They came in fifteen minutes and ten minutes after that I was at Hope and Anchor, which I had been to a few times. It was almost ten thirty in the morning. It was a faux rustic little place—a cutesy, gentrified outpost in the old waterfront neighborhood of Red Hook, which in the last five years had started attracting artists, the kinds of people who fifteen years before had been colonizing the Williamsburg neighborhood of Brooklyn, and they colonized it so well that they can't afford to live there anymore. So now it's Red Hook.

The place was empty at ten thirty in the morning on a Friday, except for a scruffy twentysomething fellow drinking coffee and reading the *New York Times,* and the waitress, a cute hippie-looking blonde, also in her twenties. I ordered a coffee. I wasn't thinking about much. I was sort of high or something. High on the folly of all that I had been doing. But not high in a good way, more like I was out of it, dazed. It didn't help that I had probably slept only about three hours.

Then G came in. He was my height, about six feet, and had a muscular V-shaped torso discernible underneath a gray sweatshirt with a hood. He had shiny black hair, which was greased back, and he was good-looking, nice features—a straight, elegant nose, big eyes, masculine chin. He had light brown skin, and, like Shiny the bartender said, was probably in his early thirties. There was a scar on his right cheek, not too pronounced but visible. We made eye contact and I didn't like the way he looked at me. My heart stopped and he came over to me, sat right next to me, instead of across from me, put a switchblade right against my belly, and said, "Let's talk outside. I'll rip you up. I don't give a shit. Just walk out with me."

"I haven't paid for my coffee," I said. Why this occurred to me, I don't know.

"Put the money on the table and fucking walk out," he said. The waitress was sitting at the bar with her back to me, and the boy with his paper didn't even look up. Music was playing loudly on the stereo system. They were in their own worlds.

I put a five on the table, it was the smallest bill I had, and G walked behind me and led me outside to a big car, a sky blue Chevy Caprice, with fancy rims. I knew it was a Caprice. I'd had one years ago. He had a friend in the front seat at the wheel and we sat in the back.

We drove a few blocks and then turned right on Coffey, which is a long block of warehouses that leads to the waterfront and the moribund, long-dead Red Hook piers. Manhattan was across the river and to the right, gleaming and rich. Straight ahead, about half a mile away, was the Statue of Liberty. It was a beautiful day out—clear and bright.

Spanish music played on the radio and they didn't say anything. I hadn't gotten too good a look at the driver, but he seemed younger than G, probably in his early twenties, and from the backseat I looked at his shiny black hair, which was cut close to his scalp, so you could see the skin between each individual hair. His neck and shoulders were fat. He was a fat boy.

"Is G your full name or just an initial?" I asked.

"Shut up," he said, and then said something in Spanish to the driver.

"Where's Lisa?" I said, pretending to be brave, and I sort of fooled myself in that I actually felt sort of brave.

"I told you to shut up."

We pulled into a garagelike warehouse, not too big, but room enough for the car and a van that was already parked and which had C & L BEVERAGES stenciled on its side. Toward the back of the garage there were dozens of piled-up cases of soda and water and beer.

We got out of the car. G pushed me toward the far-left corner, where there was a battered steel door. He stayed behind me, and I didn't feel the knife, but I knew it wasn't far away. His fat friend followed after us. We went through the door and into a crowded office that had more cases of water and soda stacked along its walls. On a little couch was Lisa Weiss, with thick gray tape over her mouth, and her wrists and ankles were also bound by tape. She was wearing a short black skirt and a white blouse, which was dirty and ripped by the right shoulder, like she had been yanked, and because of the tape around her ankles her knees were close together and prim-looking. The hollows of her eyes were darkened from exhaustion and smeared mascara, and she stared at me.

There was a battered desk next to the couch, and behind it was a squat, older man with gray in his short, close-cropped hair. He had a black moustache, also with traces of gray, and like G and the fat boy, he was Hispanic, with yellow-brown skin. He appeared to be in his midfifties and was wearing a blue short-sleeved sport shirt, with only two buttons and an open collar. He was smoking a cigarette and had a thin-lipped ugly mouth underneath his moustache. G pushed me forward so that I was standing right by the edge of the desk. The older man spoke to me.

"Where's Vincent?"

"I told G here that I found him dead last night of an overdose. At the Senton Hotel." The girl kicked out her legs, but nobody paid attention to her.

"Don't fucking lie to me," said the old man.

"I'm not, I swear . . . He had just shot up. He OD'd. I'm just looking for this girl." I pointed to Lisa. She kicked her legs again. "Her sister asked me to find her and I tracked down Vincent and found him dead."

"Are you fucking with me?" the old man asked, and G stuck me in the back with the knife, just enough so that I could feel the point coming through my sport coat.

"I'm not. I promise. I just want to take this girl and leave. I don't know what's going on."

"Your friend Vincent owes me seventy-five thousand dollars, one key. I told him he had to have it to me by *today*."

"He's not my friend."

"I gave him all the bars on Avenue B for dealing and he fucked me over. You can never trust a junkie. I have to say that it's my own damn fault." He seemed to be speaking more to G and the fat boy than to me.

"I don't know what's going on," I said. "But he's dead. I'm telling you the truth. You could call the Senton Hotel and ask them if someone died there last night. He was in room sixty-three."

The old man was quiet. "If he died, it wasn't our shit," he then said, not really to anyone.

He opened a drawer in his desk and then came around to my side. He was shorter and more squat than I realized, maybe five foot five, but there was a large black gun in his hand and so it didn't really matter. He said something to G in Spanish and G shoved me down to my knees. I don't think the old man liked me towering over him.

Then he pushed the gun against my mouth. "Open up," he said. I didn't. I glanced for a second at the girl; her eyes were terrified and she was kicking out her legs. G took a step toward her and she stopped the kicking. The old man said it again, "Open up," but I didn't. Then he smacked me across the jaw with the handle of the gun, making sure to hit the bone. I opened my mouth then and he put the gun inside. I tasted the grease and the metal.

"That bastard has nine lives. All junkies do. I don't think he's dead. He got away from these two *maricons*, jumping out a window, should have broken his neck then, and they bring me this Jewish bitch. I don't need her and I don't need you. I need Vincent. I want my money." He swirled the gun around in my mouth, knocking it gently against my teeth. I stared at his yellow hand holding the gun, his thick blunt fingers. Lisa must have been with Vincent at the apartment when G and the fat boy showed up; Vincent went out the window, left his cell phone, and they took the girl. I thought of that dog. "But he doesn't have my money," the old man went on, "and tells you to call G and act like he's dead to get out of it. So you fucking tell me where Vincent is hiding!"

"He's dead. OD'd," I said, and with the gun in my mouth I sounded horrific, like a deaf-mute, my words all strangled.

He violently raked the gun sideways out of my mouth, breaking my front teeth on purpose. I screamed and my mouth filled with blood.

Then he hit me across the face with the gun, doing it very hard this time, using the barrel like a knife and opening up my cheek.

"Is he really dead? Don't lie to me!"

"Yes. Please. Please. I'm sorry." I was begging and my mouth was bleeding, and my teeth were sharp, broken things. I put my hand to my face, to try to keep my cheek in one piece, I could feel it flapping open; I might have been going into shock, it was like I wasn't really there. I was detached and drifting away, passive and submissive. I had always wondered how so many Jews could be killed in Germany, but now I knew why they would get on their knees and be shot into their own open graves.

Then there was a spark of life in my mind, what I thought was a solution, and I said, "I went to his apartment. There was a lot of musical equipment in his bedroom. You could sell it and probably make some of your money back. I'll help you, I promise. That's probably where a lot of the money went."

My words were all mangled and came out sibilant because of my teeth, and the old man looked at me like I was crazy. Then he handed the gun to G and muttered something in Spanish, and I couldn't have possibly seen it, but I felt like I did, some kind of Darwin thing where an animal, a human animal like me, can see things it shouldn't. So I saw G swinging the gun down at the back of my head and then my head and eyes were filled with a red-orange color and there was a burning pain at the base of my neck, my spine itself was in an agony it had never felt before, and then there was blackness, like a sudden, violent suffocation.

When I came to I thought I was in a dark metal box, I couldn't really see anything, and there was something soft next to my face. I reached across myself and ran my hand over the soft thing and my eyes adjusted to the minimal light and I saw that I was touching Lisa Weiss's leg. She was still taped up and she had passed out. We were moving, and I realized I was lying in the back of what must have been the van I had seen in the garage. There were a few cases of Poland Spring water and there were two frosted-over windows on the back doors and they let in just enough milky light for me to make things out. It was a closed-off compartment, and whoever was driving the van was on the other side of the aluminum-sheet wall behind me. I touched my face. It was dried and swollen, but there was a long hole, a groove I could put my finger in. I felt horrified and I sat up. I ran my tongue over my jagged teeth and I looked at my watch. It was almost nine p.m.; I had been out for hours. I reached behind my head and felt a swelling back there that was the size of a tennis ball. I shook Lisa but she didn't wake up.

I felt for my cell phone and wallet, but they were both gone. I slid down to the doors, but there were no inside handles. I tried to look out the windows, but I couldn't see anything. I was incredibly thirsty and it seemed like odd luck that there were cases of water. I pulled a bottle out of one of the boxes and I took a sip but I could barely swallow.

We were driving somewhere very bumpy and I spilled most of the water on myself, but what little I was able to get down tasted good. I looked again at my watch. I couldn't believe how long I had been out. I figured they had waited until it was dark so that they would have the cover of night for killing us and getting rid of our bodies.

They must have followed up, after all, on what I told them about Vincent, and without him the girl was just a liability, no longer a bargaining chip, just somebody they had kidnapped, so better to get rid of her; and me, well, I was a fool that they had absolutely no use for and if I was dead, then I couldn't make trouble for them. They had a good setup: they distributed beverages and heroin, and that's probably how they met Vincent. The beverages got them in the door at bars and then they hooked up bartenders to deal for them. They dealt in two substances that people needed, and the liquids probably cleaned the cash from the drugs.

I looked around me. I didn't want to die. I had to do something to help me and this girl. In the murky shadows I made out a spare tire attached to the wall of the van. I thought maybe I could use the tire to bang open the door. It was a futile thought, but I tried to take the tire off the wall and I saw that inside it was a jack and a tire iron. I yanked out the iron. One end was shaped like an egg holder for unscrewing lug nuts, and the other end was a sharpish wedge for prying off hubcaps. The van came to a stop. I got to my feet. I could just about stand near the two doors, bending over a little. My head was pounding. I held the tire iron like a club, the lug nut end in my fist.

The doors opened up and it was the fat boy and I came down on his face with the tire iron as hard as I could and the thing went right through his nose and deep into his face and got stuck there. I fell forward and he fell back onto the ground and I landed on top of him and it was a freakish thing but that tire iron, with my weight behind it, pierced deeper into his flesh and must have gone right into his brain.

A car door slammed toward the front of the van and I scrambled around and saw that the fat boy had a gun tucked into his pants. I yanked that out, sprawling across him, my stomach on his thick legs, and G came around, talking on his cell phone, probably to a girl; he was saying, "Okay, baby," and he was five feet from me and he said, "Oh, fuck," and I had the gun pointed right at him. I pulled the trigger and nothing happened. It was on safety.

G dropped his phone and reached for his own gun, which was in a large pocket in the side of his pants, and I flipped the safety—my dad had guns when I was a kid and I knew where the safety was—and I shot at G and somehow I missed and he was bent over, struggling with the Velcro on his pocket, and I fired again and it went right through the top of his sleek black head and he went down.

I looked around me. We were near the water, the edge of the Atlantic Ocean. I could see the Verrazano Bridge to the north. We were on some bumpy, broken-up service road off the Belt Parkway. High weeds and concrete barriers hid us from view, but high-powered streetlights from the highway, about two hundred yards away, cast everything in silvery shadows and light came off the water like a mirror.

G and the fat boy were probably going to shoot us and then dump us in the current. I dropped the gun and went into the van. I shook Lisa and poured a bottle of water on her face and she still wouldn't wake up. I worried about hurting her, but I yanked off her mouth tape and vomit spilled out. I realized she was dead. She must have vomited behind that tape and choked to death.

Somehow, shifting their bodies a little at a time, I got G and his friend into the back of the van and closed them in there with Lisa. I looked for my phone on G and the fat boy, but they didn't have it, and they also didn't have my wallet. So I thought of using G's phone to call the police, but then I felt like I had to keep moving; I didn't want to wait for the cops to come to me. I started the van up, found my way out to the highway, and decided to go to my own neighborhood, to go to *my* precinct. It was some kind of muted desire to just go home, but I knew I couldn't go home just yet, so the best I could do was go to the police *near my home*.

And I knew I had to go to them. I had killed two men and I had more or less killed this girl I had never really met. If I hadn't interfered, they might have let her go. Without me bringing the news, it could have been awhile before they found out Vincent was dead, if they ever did find out, and so they probably would have just threatened her, said they'd be watching her until Vincent showed up. She'd still have value to them as a link to their money and so she'd be alive, and maybe she would have been smart and gotten far away from New York. She could have been safe. But I had complicated everything and so because of me she was dead.

I drove north on the Belt, and the lights of the oncoming traffic were killing my eyes. I knew I must have a bad concussion and I couldn't stop morbidly running my tongue over my fractured teeth, which made me think of the old man in the garage. I didn't like the fact that he probably had my phone and my wallet. Maybe I wouldn't be able to pin anything on him and he'd come after me. He could find me.

So I changed my mind and I didn't go immediately to the police. I drove over to Coffey Street and pulled into the garage. The blue Caprice was there and there was a light under the door in the corner. I don't think he was expecting me and I had the fat boy's gun in my hand.

McSweeney's Issue 24, 2007

Acknowledgments

I would like to thank Rosalie Siegel and Brant Rumble for helping put this book together, and Doug Brod, Dave Eggers, and Tom Beller for generously publishing my work.

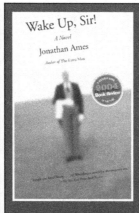